IN LOVING MEMORY OF CHESTER.

TO MY WIFE, DANA, FOR LOVINGLY ENCOURAGING ME TO NOT
QUIT MY DAY JOB; TO SAWYER AND LINCOLN, MY INSPIRATION
FOR THIS BOOK; TO MY PARENTS, FOR LETTING ME READ UNTIL THE
WEE HOURS IN THE MORNING; AND TO MY SIBLINGS, IN-LAWS, AND
FRIENDS--THANK YOU FOR YOUR SUPPORT. I LOVE YOU ALL!
-L.S.

TO MY MOM AND DAD, WHO LOVED ME IN
SPITE OF MY DIRTY DIAPERS.
-A.R.

WHY WOULD WE HAVE DEDICATIONS TO HOOMANS
WHEN WE CAN USE THIS SPACE FOR MORE
DRAWINGS OF ME?
-LINCOLN

PUBLISHED BY BLUE HOUSE PRESS, NAPA CA
COPYRIGHT 2017 LARISA STEPHENSON AND ANNIE RUYGT
NO PART OF THIS BOOK MAY BE REPRODUCED WITHOUT PERMISSION
FROM THE AUTHOR AND ILLUSTRATOR.

GIVE ME A SECOND TO BURY MY BONE SO
IT CAN MARINATE IN MY SALIVA, AND THEN
I WILL PROPERLY INTRODUCE MYSELF.

MY NAME IS LINCOLN.
AS YOU HAVE PROBABLY NOTICED, I AM AN EXTREMELY **HANDSOME** DOG. LYING IN THIS ROOM, ENJOYING A NAP THAT WILL MOST LIKELY LAST ONLY 18 MINUTES, IS MY BABY BROTHER.

SHHHH!

DON'T WAKE THE
SLEEPING DRAGON. . .

FOR THE FIRST 9 YEARS OF MY LIFE,
I ENJOYED THE LUXURY AND PERKS OF BEING
AN ONLY CHILD.

LIFE WAS GREAT!

LAST SPRING, MOMS WENT OUT OF TOWN, SO I WENT TO GRANDMA AND GRANDPA'S FOR VACATION. I HAD A MARVELOUS TIME RUNNING AROUND WITH CHESTER AND MILO, SLEEPING IN THE SUN, AND EATING AS MUCH ICE CREAM AS I COULD GET MY PAWS ON. (GRANDPA CAVES EASILY.)

A WEEK LATER, WHEN MOMS ARRIVED HOME, ONE LOOKED NOTICEABLY SKINNIER, AND SHE WAS HOLDING A BABY WITH A NEW RED STUFFED BONE ON HIS BELLY. THAT BABY WAS MY NEW HOOMAN BROTHER, AND THAT RED BONE WAS A BRIBE.

LIFE AS I KNEW IT WOULD **NEVER** BE THE SAME.

MOMS NOW SHUSH ME WHEN I BARK AT ANYONE WITHIN A 2-BLOCK RADIUS OF OUR HOUSE, REGARDLESS OF THE TIME OF DAY.

THIS IRKS ME BECAUSE IT'S OK FOR MY BROTHER TO SCREAM AND CRY ALL NIGHT LONG.

wwwaaaaaaaa !!!

DARN THOSE DOUBLE STANDARDS!!

I WOULD ALSO BECOME HURT WHEN PEOPLE WOULD COME OVER, AND I WAS NO LONGER THE CENTER OF ATTENTION.

MOMS NOTICED I WAS MORE UPSET THAN MY FIRST DEBILITATING TRIP TO THE VET, AND THEY WERE FIXIN' TO CHEER ME UP. ONE DAY, WHILE MY BROTHER WAS SLEEPING, THEY SAT DOWN ON THE COUCH WITH ME.

AS WE CUDDLED, THEY EXPLAINED THAT THEY
STILL LOVED ME JUST AS MUCH AS BEFORE, BUT THAT
MY BROTHER NEEDED A LOT OF CARING, AS HE WAS
CURRENTLY UNABLE TO DO ANYTHING FOR HIMSELF.
THEY ALSO PROMISED ME THAT THE NEAR FUTURE
WOULD HOLD A LOT OF FUN TIMES FOR US AS MY
BROTHER "GREW LIKE A WEED."

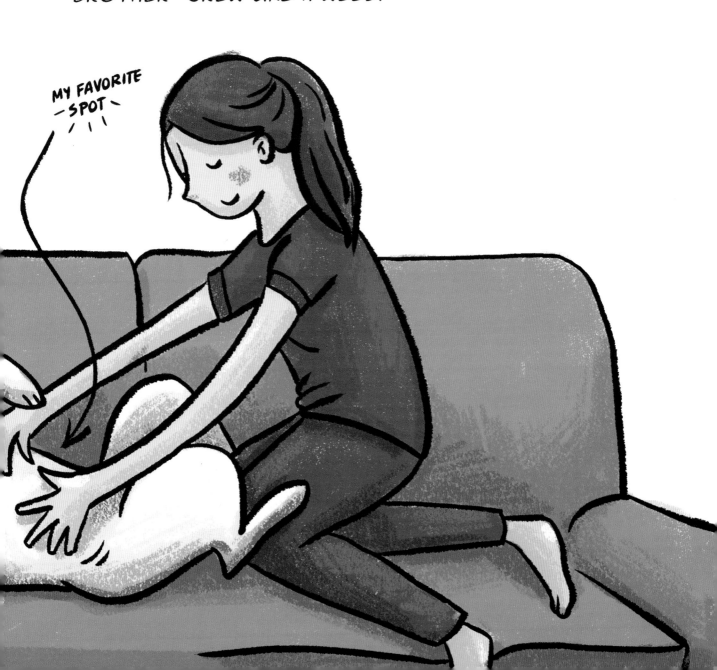

SO I WAITED,

. . . AND WATCHED.

MOMS WERE RIGHT!

BURP!

FROM THE FIRST TUMMY ROLL, MOMS AND I WORKED
HARD TO KEEP UP WITH HIM. THAT KID PICKED UP
SPEED FASTER THAN I EAT STEAK!

THERE ISN'T A DAY THAT GRAVITY
DOESN'T SHOW UP TO WORK.

I LOVED IT WHEN HE STARTED EATING MORE
INTERESTING FOODS. MY BROTHER HAS EXCELLENT
TASTE.

EACH DAY WE ARE BOTH LEARNING NEW THINGS.

I AM LEARNING HOW TO BE AN INSPIRING BIG BROTHER, AND HE IS STILL LEARNING HOW TO **NOT** HIT HIS HEAD ALL THE TIME, **NOT** FALL OFF THE COUCH, **NOT** ELECTROCUTE HIMSELF, **NOT** CHOKE ON EVERY BITE OF FOOD, AND MUCH, MUCH MORE. SOMETIMES I STILL MAKE MISTAKES, BUT WE'RE BOTH HAVING A GREAT TIME TOGETHER. I TRULY LOVE BEING A BIG BROTHER!

I WANT TO SHARE WITH YOU 3 MAJOR LESSONS I'VE LEARNED THIS YEAR.

#1 IF YOU'RE NOT READY FOR A SIBLING, DON'T GO TO GRANDMA AND GRANDPA'S FOR VACATION BECAUSE YOUR PARENTS MIGHT COME HOME WITH A BABY BROTHER, OR SISTER. . . OR BOTH!

#2 NO MATTER HOW MANY NAPS YOU TAKE, YOU CAN NEVER CATCH UP ON THE SLEEP YOU LOSE THE FIRST FEW MONTHS. BUT DON'T LET THAT STOP YOU FROM TRYING!

#3

THIS IS THE MOST IMPORTANT LESSON, ESPECIALLY IF YOU FORGET LESSON #1. KNOW THAT A SIBLING MIGHT NOT BE WHAT YOU WANTED AT FIRST, BUT IT'S TOTALLY WORTH ALL THE LOVE AND GREAT TIMES YOU WILL HAVE TOGETHER!

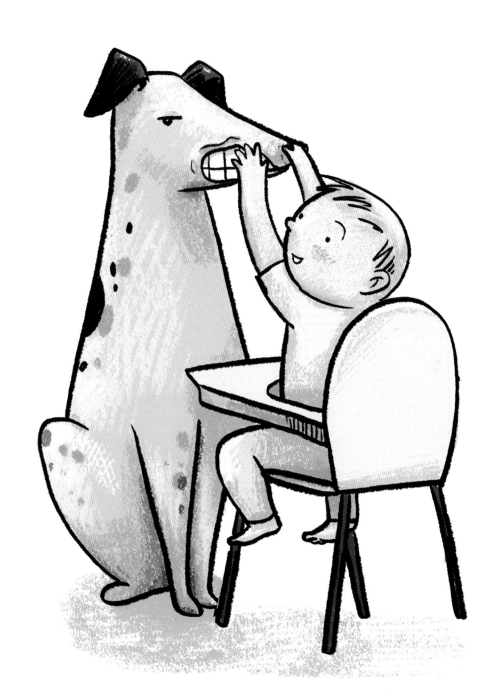

AS YOU CAN SEE, WE REALLY LOVE EACH OTHER.